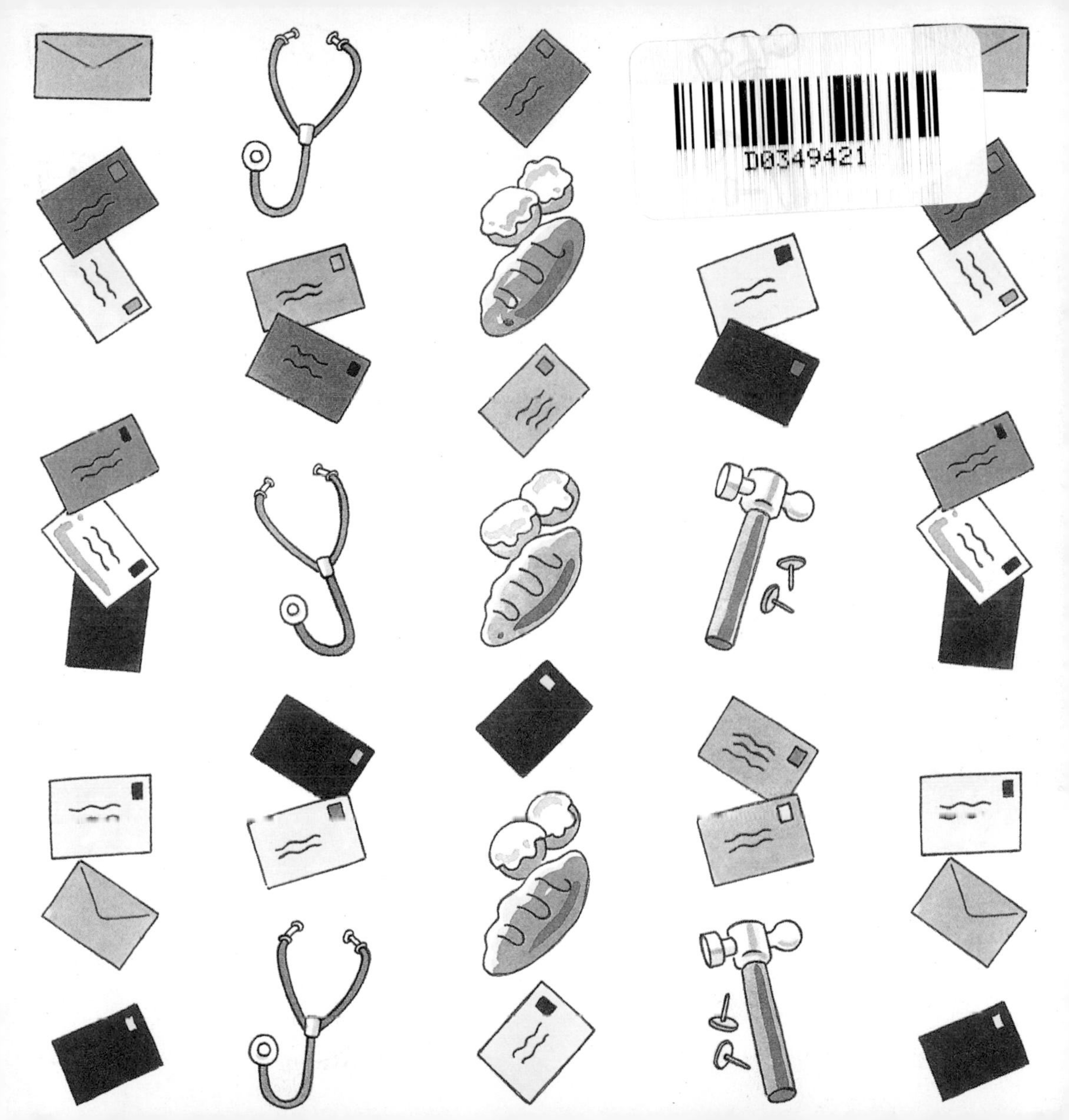

BIG BEAR'S
BUSY DAY

Written by Dugald Steer

Illustrated by John Blackman

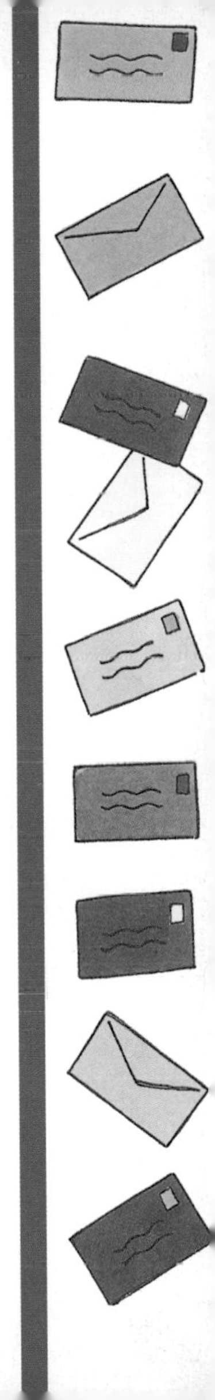

Olive Owl is a **teacher**.
She teaches in the school.
Hello, Big Bear. Hello,
Morris Mouse. The
postman is poorly.
Can you deliver
the children's
letters?

Of course,
say Big Bear
and Morris Mouse.

There are a lot of letters!
A letter for the **milkman**.

He is delivering the **milk**.

A letter for the **farmer**.
He is looking after
the **animals**.

A letter for the **carpenter**.
He is building something!

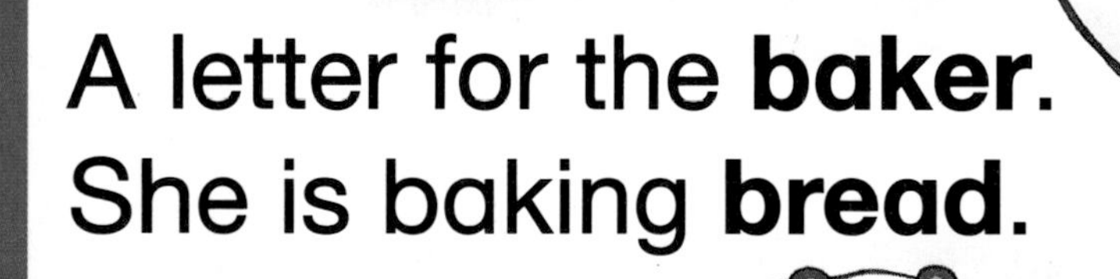

A letter for the **baker**.
She is baking **bread**.

Another for the **greengrocer**.
He is selling **fruit** and
vegetables.

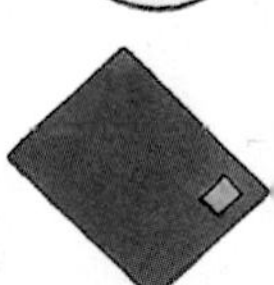

A letter for the **bus driver** and letters for her **passengers.**

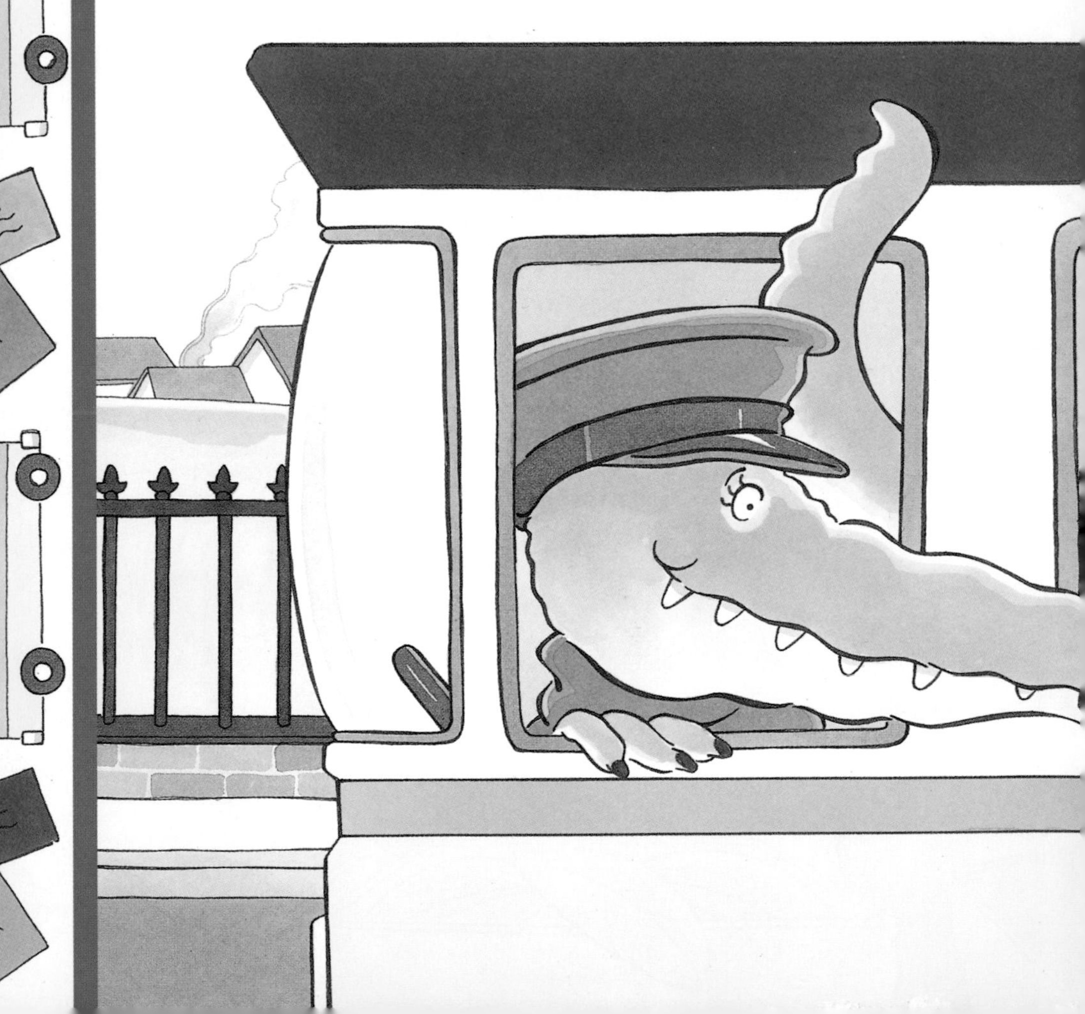

DING! DING! Hold on tight!

A letter for the **fireman**.
He is putting out a **fire**!

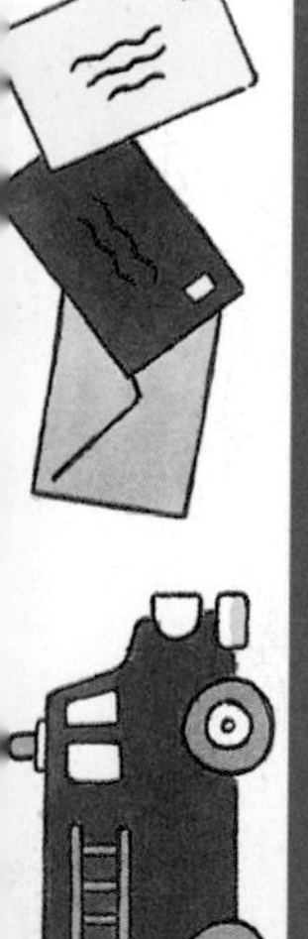

Wait a minute, Big Bear!

A letter for the **doctor**. He is looking after his **patient**.

Big Bear is tired!
What a busy day it has been!

There is one more letter.
Who do you think it is for?

Big Bear and Morris Mouse! It says:

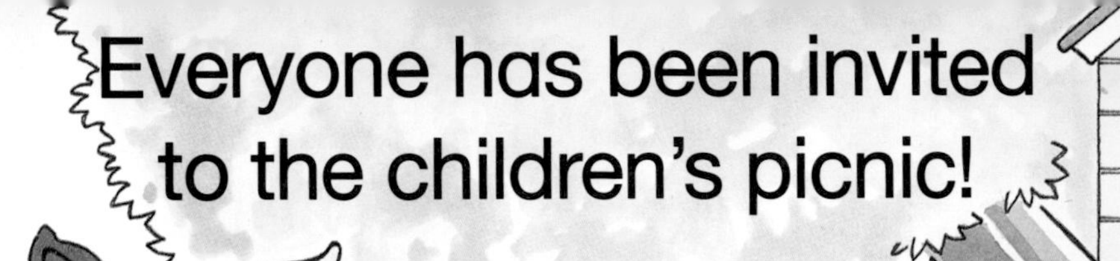

Everyone has been invited
to the children's picnic!

Thank you,
children!

This is a Parragon Book.

Parragon
13-17 Avonbridge Trading Estate,
Atlantic Road, Avonmouth, Bristol. BS11 9QD

Produced by The Templar Company plc
Pippbrook Mill, London Road, Dorking, Surrey RH4 1JE.

Designed by Janie Louise Hunt
Printed and bound in Italy
ISBN 0-75251-483-0

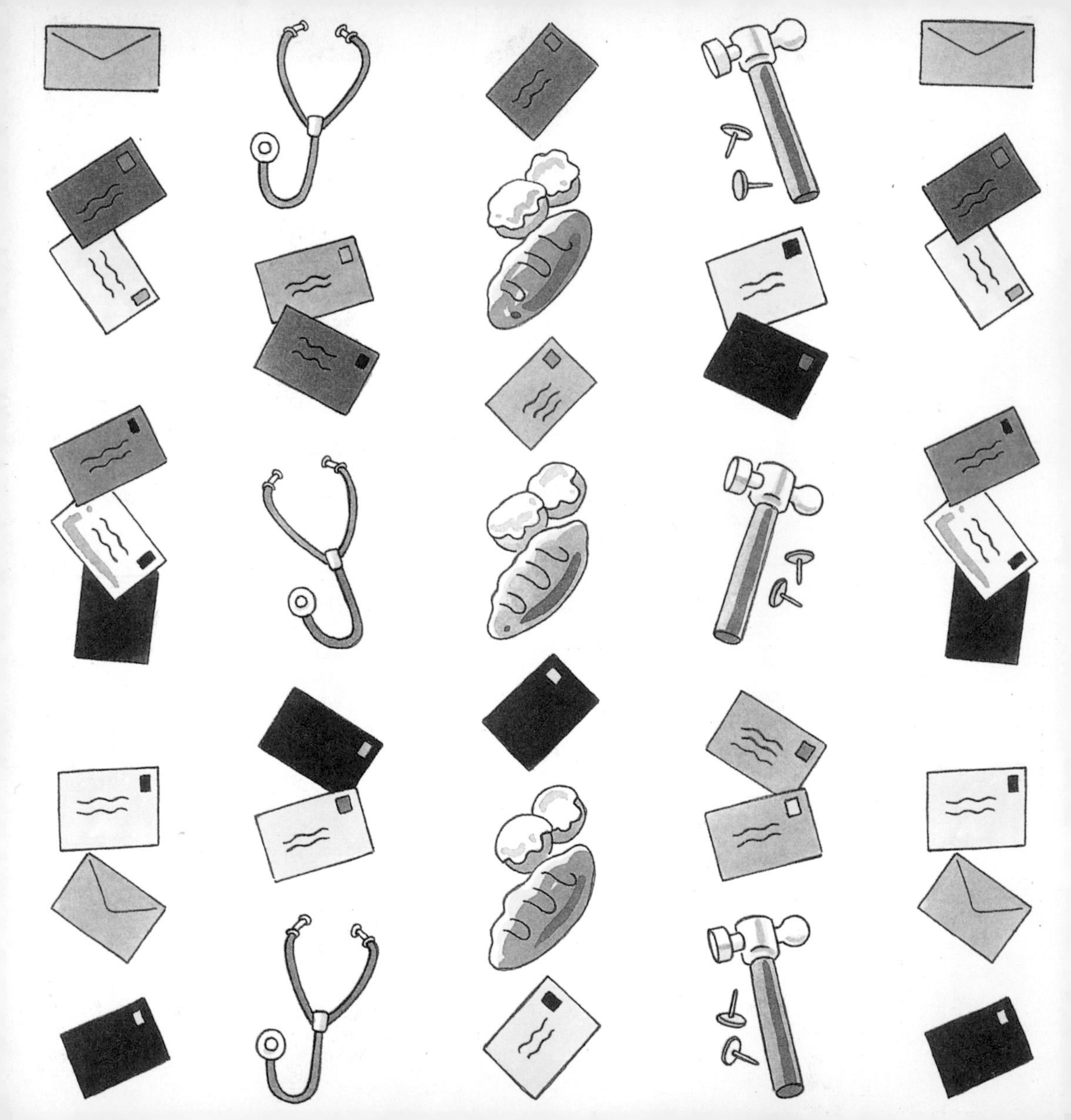